"Bring The Classics To Life"

HEIDI

LEVEL 1

Series Designer
Philip J. Solimene

Editor
Laura Machynski

EDCON
Long Island, New York

Story Adaptor
Carolyn Gloeckner

Author
Johanna Spyri

Copyright © 1995
A/V Concepts Corp.
30 Montauk Blvd., Oakdale, NY 11769

info@edconpublishing.com

Printed in U.S.A.
ISBN# 1-55576-178-X

CONTENTS

Words Used 4, 5

NO.	TITTLE	SYNOPSIS	PAGE
61	Grandfather's House	Aunt Dete takes Heidi to live with her grandfather on the Alm.	6
62	Peter	Heidi makes friends with Peter and his grandmother.	12
63	Heidi Meets Klara	Heidi leaves the Alm to live with a rich family in the city.	18
64	Kittens for Klara	Heidi brings happiness to her friend Klara.	24
65	Heidi's Book	Grandmamma helps Heidi learn how to read.	30
66	The Open Door	Heidi misses the Alm so much that she is getting sick.	36
67	Home Again	At long last, Heidi returns to the Alm.	42
68	Helping Friends	Heidi helps Peter to read.	48
69	On the Alm	Klara gets her wish to visit the Alm.	54
70	The Lost Wheel Chair	The Alm and Heidi's friendship help Klara to walk again.	60

WORDS USED

Story 61	Story 62	Story 63	Story 64	Story 65
KEY WORDS				
happy	are	ask	after	am
looked	eat	be	bring	has
new	goat	call	could	of
was	her	living	kitten	picture
your	sit	read	pocket	please
NECESSARY WORDS				
ladder	fix	chair	angry	beautiful
mountain	grandmother	city	breakfast	dirty
place	herder	rich	church	learn
supper	rattle	wheel	lessons	strange
top	wind		meow	wrong
			professor	

WORDS USED

Story 66	Story 67	Story 68	Story 69	Story 70
KEY WORDS				
must	basket	box	color	by
out	don't	can't	from	lost
spring	no	each	if	or
there	ran	tell	lunch	sat
were	us	too	yellow	three

Story 66	Story 67	Story 68	Story 69	Story 70
NECESSARY WORDS				
die	forget	fields	excited	himself
dream	held	gifts	eyes	hurt
need	rolls		forgot	left
open	sad	month	hugged	push
sick	tired	moved	later	wonderful
winter		together		

Grandfather's House

PREPARATION

Key Words

happy	(hap ´ē)	glad; pleased *We are <u>happy</u> to see you.*
looked	(lükəd)	saw; had seen *I <u>looked</u> at the picture.*
new	(nü)	not old; never owned or seen before *Mary had a <u>new</u> blue hat.*
was	(woz)	is, in the past; has been *She <u>was</u> a good little girl.*
your	(yu̇r)	owned by you *This is <u>your</u> ball.*

Grandfather's House

Necessary Words

ladder (lad´er) a set of steps for use in climbing up and down
Go up the ladder and get the balloon.

mountain (mount´n) a very high hill
Shawn lives in a house on a mountain.

place (plās) spot; site
This is a good place to live.

supper (sup´ər) the last meal of the day
Mark ate supper at John's house.

top (top) the highest place or part
Sue walked to the top of the hill.

People

Heidi is a little girl who lives in Switzerland.

Aunt Dete is Heidi's aunt.

Places

Alm a mountain in Switzerland

Grandfather's House

Aunt Dete takes Heidi to her new home.

Preview: 1. Read the name of the story.
2. Look at the picture.
3. Read the sentence under the picture.
4. Read the first five paragraphs of the story.
5. Then answer the following question.

You learned from your preview that Heidi
___a. did not like living at home.
___b. wanted to live with her grandfather.
___c. wanted to live with Aunt Dete.
___d. did not have a mother or father.

Turn to the Comprehension Check on page 10 for the right answer.

Now read the story.

Read to find out how Heidi likes her new home.

Grandfather's House

Heidi did not have a mother or father. She lived with Aunt Dete.

One day, Aunt Dete took Heidi on a long walk. The walked up a mountain. They walked a long way.

At last, they came to a little house.

Aunt Dete said, "Stop here. This is Grandfather's house. It is your new home, Heidi."

Grandfather was not happy to see them. He did not want Heidi to live with him.

He said to Aunt Dete, "She can not stay. Take her back. Take her back now!"

Aunt Dete said, "I have to go away for a while. And she can not come with me. It is time for you to have her. She is your little girl now."

Grandfather was not happy. "Let her stay, then," he said. "But I want *you* to go away. Go now Dete! I never want to see you again! Do not come back here!"

Dete hurried away down the mountain. She did not look back.

Heidi and Grandfather went into the house.

"Where will I sleep, Grandfather?" Heidi said.

"Look around for a place you like. You may sleep where you wish," said Grandfather.

Heidi looked around the house. She went up a ladder. At the top, she found a room.

"Come up and look, Grandfather!" said Heidi. "Here is a good place for my bed. From here, I can see far down the mountain."

"This mountain's name is The Alm," said Grandfather.

Heidi helped make supper. Grandfather looked at Heidi as she worked. He saw that Heidi was a happy little girl.

Soon, it was dark. Heidi went up the ladder to bed.

She liked this new home on the Alm.

Grandfather's House

COMPREHENSION CHECK

Choose the best answer.

Preview Answer:

   d. did not have a mother or father.

1. In the beginning of this story, Heidi was living with her
   _____a. grandmother.
   _____b. sister.
   _____c. brother.
   _____d. Aunt Dete.

2. Heidi went to live with her grandfather because
   _____a. Aunt Dete didn't like Heidi any more.
   _____b. Aunt Dete had to go away for a while.
   _____c. Grandfather missed Heidi.
   _____d. Heidi didn't want to live with Aunt Dete.

3. Grandfather
   _____a. was a young man.
   _____b. was an old man.
   _____c. was a tall man.
   _____d. was a small man.

4. Grandfather lived
   _____a. in a big city.
   _____b. in a small town.
   _____c. on a mountain.
   _____d. under the ground.

5. Grandfather
   _____a. was not happy to see Aunt Dete and Heidi.
   _____b. was very glad to see them.
   _____c. never liked Heidi.
   _____d. loved Heidi more than anyone.

6. Grandfather let Heidi stay. But he was
   _____a. angry with Aunt Dete.
   _____b. sad for Aunt Dete.
   _____c. pleased with Aunt Dete.
   _____d. afraid of Heidi.

7. At Grandfather's house, you could get to Heidi's room by
   _____a. digging a hole.
   _____b. going up a tree.
   _____c. going down a ladder.
   _____d. going up a ladder.

8. Heidi
   _____a. missed her Aunt Dete.
   _____b. liked her new home.
   _____c. did not like her new home.
   _____d. did not like Grandfather.

9. Another name for this story could be
   _____a. "Heidi Runs Away."
   _____b. "A New Home For Heidi."
   _____c. "Heidi Makes Supper."
   _____d. "The Mountain House."

10. This story is mainly about
   _____a. a girl who goes to live with her grandfather.
   _____b. an old man who does not like children.
   _____c. a beautiful mountain home.
   _____d. a girl who likes to cook.

Check your answers with the key on page 67.

Grandfather's House

VOCABULARY CHECK

happy	looked	new	was	your

I. Sentences to Finish

Fill in the blank in each sentence with the correct key word from the box above.

1. Maria was so_____to be going to the party.

2. Linda got her_____dress all dirty.

3. Who is older? You or_____brother?

4. I_____at the clock to see what the time was.

5. It_____Bobby's turn to go first.

II. Making sense of Sentences

Put a check next to YES if the sentence makes sense. Put a check next to NO if the sentence does not make sense.

1. Billy <u>was</u> ten years old next year. _____YES _____NO

2. The <u>new</u> car was washed today. _____YES _____NO

3. Mother <u>looked</u> all around for her keys. _____YES _____NO

4. Tom was <u>happy</u> that he lost his bike. _____YES _____NO

5. Ken <u>was</u> not happy that he missed the game. _____YES _____NO

Check your answers with the key on page 69.

This page may be reproduced for classroom use.

Peter

PREPARATION

Key Words

are	(är)	a state of being
		You are a good girl. We are going. You are next.
eat	(ēt)	take in food
		Rosa will eat the cookie I gave her.
goat	(gōt)	an animal with horns that gives milk
		This goat is eating grass.
her	(hër)	1. belonging to, or owned by a female
		This is her dog.
		2. a word that stands for a female
		I will talk to her.
sit	(sit)	to rest on one's bottom
		Joe asked Molly to sit down

Peter

Necessary Words

fix   (fiks)   repair; make good as new
                                        Will you fix this broken toy?

grandmother   (grand´ muŦH ´ər)   the mother of one's mother or father
                                        Tom's grandmother gave him a book.

herder   (hėr´ dər)   a person who watches over animals like sheep or
                                        goats as they walk around and eat
                                        Jim was a sheep herder.

rattle   (rat´ l)   to shake so as to make noise
                                        Don't rattle the things in that box.

wind   (wind)   air moving outside
                                        The wind came and it began to rain.

People

Peter   is a boy who herds goats.

Peter

Heidi and Peter feed the goats.

Preview: 1. Read the name of the story.
2. Look at the picture.
3. Read the sentence under the picture.
4. Read the first three paragraphs of the story.
5. Then answer the following question.

You learned from your preview that Peter took care of

___a. coats.
___b. boats.
___c. goats.
___d. Heidi's grandfather.

Turn to the Comprehension Check on page 16 for the right answer.

Now read the story.

Read to find out how Heidi helps Peter's family.

Peter

Every day, Peter came to Grandfather's house. He was the goat herder. He took the goats up the mountain to eat. He stayed with them all day.

"Heidi, go with Peter," Grandfather said. "You can help him with the goats. Take something with you to eat."

So Heidi went along. It was fun!

Heidi liked Peter. He liked her. From then on, she went with him and the goats.

One day, Heidi went home with Peter. She went to see his grandmother.

Grandmother said, "So, you are Heidi. You are the girl who helps Peter. Sit here. Talk to me. Do you like living on the mountain?"

"Yes. I like it," Heidi said. "Grandfather is good to me." They had a long talk.

Heidi liked to sit and talk with Grandmother. But she did not like Grandmother's house. She heard the wind coming in.

"I hear a noise. Your house rattles," Heidi said.

"It is the wind! I can not fix it," said Grandmother.

"I will talk to Grandfather," said Heidi. "He will come and fix your house."

Heidi went home. She told Grandfather about the noise. She told him about the wind coming in. She said, "Would you do something to help? Would you fix it?"

"Yes. I will help," said Grandfather. He went to Peter's house. He fixed the places where the wind came in.

Peter's grandmother was happy. "You are a big help," she said. "Thank you, Heidi!"

Peter

COMPREHENSION CHECK

Choose the best answer.

1. Peter came to Grandfather's house
   _____a. once a week.
   _____b. once a year.
   _____c. every Sunday.
   _____d. every day.

2. Peter took the goats up the mountain
   _____a. to eat.
   _____b. to play.
   _____c. to sleep.
   _____d. to get a drink.

3. One day Heidi went with Peter and the goats because
   _____a. she liked Peter.
   _____b. she did not like Peter.
   _____c. she wanted to get away from Grandfather.
   _____d. she had no one else to play with.

4. Heidi and Peter
   _____a. had fun every day.
   _____b. did not see much of each other.
   _____c. did not get along.
   _____d. would fight about the goats.

5. One day Heidi went home with Peter. She told his grandmother that
   _____a. she did not like living with Grandfather.
   _____b. she liked living on the Alm.
   _____c. it was too cold on the Alm.
   _____d. she missed her old friends.

Preview Answer:

c. goats.

---

6. Heidi liked to
   _____a. make fun of Grandmother.
   _____b. talk with Grandmother.
   _____c. cook for Grandmother.
   _____d. take walks with Grandmother.

7. When Heidi heard the wind coming through Grandmother's house,
   _____a. she laughed.
   _____b. she put on her coat.
   _____c. she fixed the places where the wind came in.
   _____d. she asked Grandfather if he would fix Grandmother's house.

8. Heidi
   _____a. only cared about herself.
   _____b. was a kind, young girl.
   _____c. did not get along with others.
   _____d. did not get along with old people.

9. Another name for this story could be
   _____a. "Heidi Helps a Friend."
   _____b. "Heidi Has Fun."
   _____c. "A Talk With Grandmother."
   _____d. "The Wind."

10. This story is mainly about
    _____a. Peter's old grandmother.
    _____b. fixing Grandmother's house.
    _____c. a kind, young girl who helps others.
    _____d. the fun Peter and Heidi have together.

Check your answers with the key on page 67.

This page may be reproduced for classroom use.

Peter

VOCABULARY CHECK

are	eat	goat	her	sit

I. Sentences to Finish
Fill in the blank in each sentence with the correct key word from the box above.

1. Sally did not want to give_____doll away.

2. Our family sits down to _____ breakfast every morning.

3. "Where _____ you going?" asked Mother.

4. Mother told the children to _____down.

5. My pet_____ran away the other day.

II. Using the Words
On the lines below, write five of your own sentences using the key words from the box above. Use each word once, drawing a line under the key word.

1. _____

2, _____

3, _____

4. _____

5. _____

Check your answers with the key on page 69.

Heidi Meets Klara

PREPARATION

Key Words

ask	(ask)	to talk so as to question; try to find out by words *Did he <u>ask</u> for your name?*
be	(bē)	He will <u>be</u> here today. She tries to <u>be</u> good. I will <u>be</u> six years old. *Will this <u>be</u> a funny story?*
call	(kôl)	to give a name to *John asked us to <u>call</u> him Jack.*
living	(liv ´ing)	staying at a place all the time *Rose is <u>living</u> in her new house.*
read	(rēd)	to see and know words *I will <u>read</u> this book to you.*

Heidi Meets Klara

Necessary Words

chair   (char)   a seat with a back
                                   Peter will sit in my <u>chair</u>.

city   (sit´ ē)   a place where many people live and work
                                   The <u>city</u> where I live is New York.

rich   (rich)   having a lot of money
                                   <u>Rich</u> people live in big houses.

wheel   (hwēl)   a round frame that turns on its center
                                   Can you fix the <u>wheel</u> on my bike?

People

Adelheid   is Heidi's full name.

Klara   is a rich little girl who can not walk.

Miss Rottenmeier   is the woman who looks after Klara.

Mr. Sesemann   is Klara's father.

Heidi Meets Klara

Heidi leaves the Alm. She will miss her home.

Preview:
1. Read the name of the story.
2. Look at the picture.
3. Read the sentences under the picture.
4. Read the first five paragraphs of the story.
5. Then answer the following question.

You learned from your preview that Grandfather

___a. did not like Heidi.
___b. did not like Peter.
___c. did not want Heidi to go.
___d. wanted Heidi to go away.

Turn to the Comprehension Check on page 22 for the right answer.

Now read the story.

Read to find out what Heidi's real name is.

Heidi Meets Klara

Heidi liked living with Grandfather. She liked Peter and she liked the mountains. She was a happy little girl.

One day, Aunt Dete came back. She talked to Grandfather. "I have come to ask you something. Will you let Heidi come with me? I have found her a new home. She will be living with rich people. She will be a friend for their little girl."

"Rich people! Heidi likes it here. She will stay with me," said Grandfather.

Aunt Dete talked to him for a long time. "Heidi will go to school. This is a good thing for her."

At last, Grandfather gave in. "Take her. But do not come back here again."

At first, Heidi would not go.

Aunt Dete said, "You may come back any time you wish."

So Heidi went with her. They went on the train. They went to a house in the city. It was Mr. Sesemann's home.

Mr. Sesemann had a little girl named Klara. He was away. Miss Rottenmeier was there with Klara. Klara was sitting in a wheel chair. She could not walk.

"What is your name?" Miss Rottenmeier asked Heidi.

"Heidi."

"That name will not do," said Miss Rottenmeier.

Aunt Dete said, "Her name is Adelheid. That is the name her mother gave her."

Miss Rottenmeier said, "Good. That is what we will call her. Do you like books, Adelheid?"

"No," said Heidi. "I can not read at all."

"Not at all?" Miss Rottenmeier looked surprised. "She can not read! She is not the girl we asked for!"

Aunt Dete said, "I have to go now." She went away. Miss Rottenmeier went along to talk to her.

Klara asked, "What do you want me to call you?"

"Call me Heidi."

Heidi Meets Klara

COMPREHENSION CHECK

Choose the best answer.

1. Aunt Dete wanted Heidi to
   _____a. stay with Grandfather.
   _____b. live with a friend.
   _____c. go to school.
   _____d. go to work.

2. Grandfather wanted Heidi
   _____a. to go away with Aunt Dete.
   _____b. to go live with rich people.
   _____c. to stay with him on the Alm.
   _____d. to live with another young girl.

3. Grandfather
   _____a. had grown to love Heidi.
   _____b. liked rich people.
   _____c. did not like little girls.
   _____d. did not believe in school.

4. Heidi
   _____a. did not want to live with rich people.
   _____b. did not want to make a new friend.
   _____c. did not want to go to school.
   _____d. did not want to leave Grandfather.

5. Heidi went by train to her new home
   _____a. in the mountains.
   _____b. in the city.
   _____c. in the woods.
   _____d. in the country.

6. Mr. Sesemann had a little girl named
   _____a. Katy
   _____b. Klara
   _____c. Kathy
   _____d. Kitty

7. Klara could not
   _____a. walk.
   _____b. talk.
   _____c. play.
   _____d. smile.

8. Heidi's real name was
   _____a. Abby.
   _____b. Alice.
   _____c. Allison.
   _____d. Adelheid.

9. Another name for this story could be
   _____a. "Heidi's New Friend."
   _____b. "Heidi's New Home."
   _____c. "Grandfather Gives In."
   _____d. "Living in the City."

10. This story is mainly about
    _____a. a young girl who is sent to a new home so she can have a better life.
    _____b. a young girl who makes a new friend.
    _____c. a young girl who has no friends.
    _____d. a young girl who wanted to live in the city.

Check your answers with the key on page 67.

This page may be reproduced for classroom use.

Heidi Meets Klara

VOCABULARY CHECK

ask	be	call	living	read

I. Sentences to Finish

Fill in the blank in each sentence with the correct key word from the box above.

1. We have a rabbit_____in our yard.

2. Martha will_____ten years old this year.

3. I love to_____books about animals.

4. I will_____Ida if she can sleep over my house today.

5. Jane will_____her new dog "Rusty."

II. Matching

Write the letter of the correct meaning from Column B next to the key word in Column A.

Column A	Column B
_____1. ask	a. staying at a place all the time
_____2. be	b. to give a name to
_____3. call	c. to talk so as to question; find out by words
_____4. living	d. He will_____here. I will_____six today.
_____5. read	e. to see and know words

Check your answers with the key on page 69.

This page may be reproduced for classroom use.

Kittens for Klara

PREPARATION

Key Words

after	(af´ter)	at a later time *We went to school <u>after</u> breakfast.*
bring	(bring)	come with some thing or person from another place *Can you <u>bring</u> me my balloon?*
could	(kùd)	can (if you are able) <u>*Could*</u> *you get me a cookie?*
kitten	(kit´n)	a baby cat *Carol had a new pet <u>kitten</u>.*
pocket	(pok´it)	a place to carry things in one's clothes *Put your money in your <u>pocket</u>.*

Kittens for Klara

Necessary Words

angry   (ang´grē)   cross; mad
          David was <u>angry</u> when Cary took his ball.

breakfast   (brek´fəst)   first meal of the day
          We had milk with <u>breakfast</u>.

church   (chėrch)   a place for worship
          Joe went to <u>church</u> last night.

lessons   (les´ns)   things people learn
          Mr. Green's reading <u>lessons</u> are fun.

meow   (mē ou´)   the sound a cat or kitten makes
          Gina's cat said, "<u>Meow</u>."

professor   (prə fes´ər)   teacher
          The <u>professor</u> told us about snow and rain.

Kittens for Klara

Heidi looks for the Alm, but it is gone!

Preview: 1. Read the name of the story.
2. Look at the picture.
3. Read the sentence under the picture.
4. Read the first paragraph of the story.
5. Then answer the following question.

You learned from your preview that Heidi went to the window to look for
___a. the Alm.
___b. her grandfather.
___c. Peter.
___d. Aunt Dete.

Turn to the Comprehension Check on page 28 for the right answer.

Now read the story.

Read to find out what Heidi finds in the church.

Kittens for Klara

It was morning. Heidi was in her room in Klara's house. She went to the window. She looked for the Alm. All she could see was other houses.

Heidi went to have breakfast with Klara. The girls talked and talked. Heidi told Klara about the Alm, Grandfather, and the goats.

The professor came after breakfast. He helped Klara with her school lessons. He helped IIeidi with reading.

After their lessons, Klara went to her room.

Heidi went outside. She wanted to go where she could see the Alm. She asked a boy to help her. He took her to a church. A man came to the door.

"I want to go up to the church's top," said Heidi.

"Come up, then," said the man.

They went up and up, up many steps. Heidi looked for the Alm. She could not see it -- just house tops.

On her way down, she saw a kitten. Then she saw more kittens, and their mother.

"Would you like to have them?" asked the man.

"Yes! Yes!" said IIeidi. "They will make Klara so happy."

"I will bring them. Where do you live?" asked the man.

"At Mr. Sesemann's house." she said. "I can bring two with me. I will put one in each pocket."

When Heidi got back, Miss Rottenmeier was angry. "You went out without asking. This will not do!" she said.

"Meow."

"Adelheid!" Now she was very angry.

"Meow. Meow."

Klara said, "Heidi, stop."

"But it is not me! It is the kittens in my pockets!" said Heidi. "They are for you."

"Kittens! Let me see!" cried Klara. "Look! How pretty they are!"

The other kittens came the next day. Miss Rottenmeier was not happy about it. But Klara and Heidi liked them very much.

Kittens for Klara

COMPREHENSION CHECK

Choose the best answer.

1. Klara did not go to school because
   _____a. she did not like school.
   _____b. she did not know how to get there.
   _____c. Miss Rottenmeier would not let her go.
   _____d. she was in a wheel chair.

2. Who helped Klara with her school lessons at home?
   _____a. Miss Rottenmeier
   _____b. Mr. Sesemann
   _____c. The professor
   _____d. Heidi

3. Heidi went to the church to
   _____a. look for her dog.
   _____b. find a friend.
   _____c. look for Grandfather.
   _____d. look for the Alm.

4. At the church, Heidi found
   _____a. some kittens.
   _____b. some puppies.
   _____c. some birds.
   _____d. some ants.

5. How many kittens did Heidi take home?
   _____a. One
   _____b. Two
   _____c. Three
   _____d. Five

6. Miss Rottenmeier was angry that Heidi
   _____a. went to church.
   _____b. went out without asking.
   _____c. brought home two kittens.
   _____d. came to live with the Sesemanns.

7. Klara liked
   _____a. the kittens.
   _____b. her wheelchair.
   _____c. that Miss Rottenmeier was angry.
   _____d. that Heidi went to church.

8. Miss Rottenmeier was not happy
   _____a. that Heidi and Klara got along.
   _____b. that Klara liked the kittens.
   _____c. when the professor came the next day.
   _____d. when the other kittens came the next day.

9. Another name for this story could be
   _____a. "Kittens In Pockets."
   _____b. "Miss Rottenmeier Gets Angry."
   _____c. "Breakfast With Klara."
   _____d. "Heidi Goes to Church."

10. This story is mainly about
    _____a. a girl who likes kittens.
    _____b. a girl who likes to go to church.
    _____c. a girl who tries to make her friend happy.
    _____d. a girl who makes her friend sad.

Check your answers with the key on page 67.

This page may be reproduced for classroom use.

Kittens for Klara

VOCABULARY CHECK

after	bring	could	kitten	pocket

I. Sentences to Finish
Fill in the blank in each sentence with the correct key word from the box above.

1. Mother gave us ice cream_____supper.

2. I_____lunch to school every day.

3. Sandy put her money in her_____.

4. A little gray_____followed me home today.

5. Joe asked Mike if he_____come to the game.

II. Matching
Write the letter of the correct meaning from Column B next to the key word in Column A

Column A	Column B
____1. after	a. a baby cat
____2. bring	b. a place to carry things in one's clothes
____3. could	c. at a later time
____4. kitten	d. can (if you are able)
____5. pocket	e. come with some thing or person from another place

Check your answers with the key on page 70.

This page may be reproduced for classroom use.

Heidi's Book

PREPARATION

Key Words

am   (am)   being
> *I <u>am</u> a very good girl. I <u>am</u> happy. I <u>am</u> five years old.*

has   (haz)   to hold or own
> *The dog <u>has</u> her ball.*

of   (ov)   belonging to
> *I made the man out <u>of</u> snow.*

picture   (pik´chər)   a likeness, painting or drawing
> *This is a <u>picture</u> of your grandmother.*

please   (plēz)   a way of saying, "if you would be so kind" or "if you are willing"
> *<u>Please</u> give me a cookie.*

Heidi's Book

Necessary Words

beautiful   (bū´tə fəl)   very pretty
What a <u>beautiful</u> flower!

dirty   (dėr´tē)   not clean
His hands were <u>dirty</u>.

learn   (lėrn)   understand
I want to <u>learn</u> how to fish.

strange   (strānj)   odd; different
This is such a <u>strange</u> place.

wrong   (rông)   not right
Tina was <u>wrong</u> when she said Jane was going home.

People

Grandmamma   is Klara's grandmother; Mr. Sesemann's mother

Heidi's Book

Klara tells her father not to send Heidi away. "We have such good times," she said.

Preview:
    1. Read the name of the story.
    2. Look at the picture.
    3. Read the sentences under the picture.
    4. Read the first five paragraphs of the story.
    5. Then answer the following question.

You learned from your preview that Miss Rottenmeier was not happy with

___a. Mr. Sesemann.
___b. Klara.
___c. Heidi.
___d. Aunt Dete.

Turn to the Comprehension Check on page 34 for the right answer.

Now read the story.

Read to find out how Grandmamma helps Heidi to read.

Heidi's Book

Mr. Sesemann came home. Miss Rottenmeier went to talk to him.

"I am not happy with Adelheid. Not at all! She has such strange ways! And those animals!"

"What animals?" asked Mr. Sesemann.

"She got them from a man at the church. They are so dirty!"

Mr. Sesemann talked to Klara about this. "Now Klara, what is this about Heidi? Has she some animals?" he asked.

"She has kittens, Father," said Klara. "I am happy to play with them."

"Do you want me to send Heidi away?" Mr. Sesemann asked.

"Oh, no," said Klara. "Please let her stay! She is so funny! We have such good times!"

Soon, Mr. Sesemann had to go away again. Klara's grandmother came to stay with the girls.

"Please call me Grandmamma," she said to Heidi. "I brought you a book to read."

"She can not read," said Miss Rottenmeier. "The professor tries to help her read. Little good it does."

Grandmamma looked at the book with Heidi. They came to a picture of a herder with some goats.

Heidi began to cry. She said, "It is a beautiful picture. It makes me think of Peter, and home." How Heidi missed Grandfather and the Alm!

Grandmamma said, "Heidi, work hard at your lessons. When you can read this book, I will give it to you. It will be all yours."

Heidi was surprised. "But I can not learn to read. Peter told me so."

Grandmamma laughed. "What a strange boy! I think he is wrong. You can learn to read if you try!"

She did try. Soon, she could read. And the beautiful book was hers.

Heidi's Book

COMPREHENSION CHECK

Choose the best answer.

Preview Answer:

c. Heidi.

1. Miss Rottenmeier
   _____a. waw a bad woman.
   _____b. was a happy woman.
   _____c. did not like animals.
   _____d. did not like the man who gave Heidi the kittens.

2. Klara told her father
   _____a. to send the kittens away.
   _____b. to send Heidi away.
   _____c. to let Heidi stay.
   _____d. to send Heidi to her room.

3. When Mr. Sesemann went away,
   _____a. Klara's aunt came to stay with the girls.
   _____b. Klara's grandmother came to stay with the girls.
   _____c. Klara's brother came to stay with the girls.
   _____d. Klara's uncle came to stay with the girls.

4. Grandmamma brought Heidi
   _____a. a basket for the kittens.
   _____b. some candy.
   _____c. some ice cream.
   _____d. a book.

5. Heidi
   _____a. did not like books.
   _____b. did not like Grandmamma.
   _____c. did not know how to read.
   _____d. did not know how to play.

6. When Grandmamma looked at the book with Heidi,
   _____a. Heidi began to cry.
   _____b. Heidi began to laugh.
   _____c. Heidi threw the book on the floor.
   _____d. Heidi ran to her room.

7. Heidi cried because
   _____a. she did not know how to read.
   _____b. she did not like the book.
   _____c. she did not like Grandmamma.
   _____d. a picture in the book made her think of home.

8. Grandmamma told Heidi
   _____a. to stop crying.
   _____b. to work hard at her lessons.
   _____c. to go to her room.
   _____d. she could not have the book.

9. Another name for this story could be
   _____a. "Heidi Learns to Read."
   _____b. "Heidi Gets a Book."
   _____c. "Miss Rottenmeier's Strange Ways."
   _____d. "Missing Peter."

10. This story is mainly about
    _____a. how Grandmamma and hard work helped Heidi to read.
    _____b. why Miss Rottenmeier did not like Heidi.
    _____c. how Klara and Heidi got along.
    _____d. how much Heidi missed Grandfather.

Check your answers with the key on page 67.

This page may be reproduced for classroom use.

Heidi's Book

VOCABULARY CHECK

am	has	of	picture	please

I. Sentences to Finish

Fill in the blank in each sentence with the correct key word from the box above.

1. Miss Brooks asked me to_____sit down.

2. We will all have our_____taken today.

3. Joe's boat is made out_____wood.

4. I_____happy to help Dad with the yard.

5. Lisa_____a new dress.

II. Word Search

All the words from the box above are hidden in the puzzle below. They may be written from left to right, or up and down. As you find each word, put a circle around it. One word, that is not a key word, has been done for you.

```
A  C  D  P  L  E  A  S  E
M  P  L  I  Q  R  F  C  O
H  B  O  C  H  I  N  E  F
A  H  G  T  A  X  M  A  A
T  A  H  U  S  V  O  L  R
U  E  L  R  N  G  Z  Q  T
S  T  T  E  X  P  P  O  B
```

Check your answers with the key on page 70.

This page may be reproduced for classroom use.

The Open Door

PREPARATION

Key Words

must	(must)	should; ought to *I <u>must</u> make my bed every morning.*
out	(out)	away from inside something *The children will get <u>out</u> of the water.*
spring	(spring)	the season that comes after winter *In the <u>spring</u>, new plants grow.*
there	(ŦHãr)	in that place *We looked <u>there</u> for her doll.*
were	(wėr)	had been *John and Dana <u>were</u> at the park.*

The Open Door

Necessary Words

die   (dī)   to stop living
The dog is so sick he may <u>die</u>.

dream   (drēm)   thoughts or pictures in one's sleep
Jim had a <u>dream</u> last night that he could fly.

needed   (nēd´əd)   wanted very much
I <u>needed</u> your help last night.

open   (o´pən)   not shut or closed
The door was <u>open</u>.

sick   (sik)   ill; not well
Tammy was <u>sick</u>, but now she's better.

winter   (win´tər)   the coldest season of the year
In the <u>winter</u>, we play in the snow.

People

Dr. Classen   is Mr. Sesemann's friend.

The Open Door

Heidi is very sad. She can not go back home.

Preview: 1. Read the name of the story.
2. Look at the picture.
3. Read the sentences under the picture.
4. Read the first paragraph of the story.
5. Then answer the following question.

You learned from your preview that Heidi's new book made her think of
___a. Klara.
___b. Aunt Dete.
___c. church.
___d. home.

Turn to the Comprehension Check on page 40 for the right answer.

Now read the story.

Read to find out who Heidi could not stop thinking about.

The Open Door

Heidi's new book made her think of home. Aunt Dete had said she could go back there at any time. She knew it was not so. Aunt Dete had said it to make her come here. She must stay with Klara. She could not go back home.

Klara could not run and play like other children. She needed a friend. But Heidi missed the Alm. She missed Grandfather. She missed Peter and the goats. And she missed Grandmother.

Grandmother was so old. If she got sick, she could die! Heidi could not stop thinking about her.

She looked at the book more and more. She cried in her bed at night. She stopped eating.

At last, winter was over. It was spring again. Strange things were going on in the Sesemann house.

Every morning, the door was open. No one ever saw who was going in or out. Miss Rottenmeier sent a letter to Mr. Sesemann.

Mr. Sesemann came home. He called for his old friend, Dr. Classen, to come. That night, they stayed up. The wanted to learn how the door came to be open.

Then they saw Heidi! She was walking in her sleep. She came down and went out.

They cried out in surprise. Heidi just looked at them.

"Why have you come down here?" asked Mr. Sesemann.

"I do not know." Heidi was just as surprised as they were.

Dr. Classen asked, "Did you have a dream?"

"Yes. I have the same dream every night. I am with Grandfather, on the Alm. It is spring. I jump up and run to the door. But then I am back here. The dream is over." Heidi began to cry.

When Heidi was back in bed, the two men talked. Dr. Classen said, "Heidi misses her home. It is making her sick. You must send her back there -- right away."

The Open Door

COMPREHENSION CHECK

Choose the best answer.

1. Aunt Dete had told Heidi she could go back to the Alm at any time. She said this to
   _____a. make Heidi laugh.
   _____b. make Heidi cry.
   _____c. make Heidi sad.
   _____d. make Heidi go to the Sesemanns'.

2. Heidi missed
   _____a. Grandfather.
   _____b. Grandmother.
   _____c. Peter and the Goats.
   _____d. all of the above.

3. Heidi worried a lot about Grandmother because
   _____a. Grandmother missed Heidi.
   _____b. Grandmother was very sick.
   _____c. Grandmother was very old.
   _____d. Grandmother was leaving the Alm.

4. Heidi missed the Alm so much that
   _____a. she was making herself sick.
   _____b. she would not do her work.
   _____c. she would eat too much.
   _____d. she ran away from the Sesemanns'.

5. Miss Rottenmeier sent a letter to Mr. Sesemann to tell him that
   _____a. someone had locked her out of the house.
   _____b. she found the door open every morning.
   _____c. Heidi was not being a good girl.
   _____d. Heidi was making Klara very sad.

Preview Answer:

d. home.

---

6. Mr. Sesemann and Dr. Classen found Heidi
   _____a. talking in her sleep.
   _____b. walking in her sleep.
   _____c. sleeping in Klara's bed.
   _____d. sleeping on the floor.

7. Heidi
   _____a. had a bad dream every night.
   _____b. had a funny dream every night.
   _____c. had the same dream every night.
   _____d. did not dream at all.

8. Dr. Classen said that Heidi should go back home
   _____a. in the winter.
   _____b. in the summer.
   _____c. when she was done with her lessons.
   _____d. right away.

9. Another name for this story could be
   _____a. "Sleep-walking."
   _____b. "Heidi's Surprise."
   _____c. "Heidi Misses Home."
   _____d. "Heidi's Dream."

10. This story is mainly about
    _____a. a girl who has a dream every night.
    _____b. a girl who becomes very sick.
    _____c. a girl who would not do her work.
    _____d. a girl who misses her home very much.

Check your answers with the key on page 67.

This page may be reproduced for classroom use.

The Open Door

VOCABULARY CHECK

must	out	spring	there	were

I. Sentences to Finish
Fill in the blank in each sentence with the correct key word from the box above.

1. I love the beach. We are going_____today.

2. Mother and Father_____late for the show.

3. Dad said I_____rake the leaves on Saturday.

4. In the_____, we will start a garden.

5. When I opened the door, the cat ran_____of the house.

II. In the blank space in each sentence, write the correct key word that means the same as the words under the line.

1 I was asked to go the the party, but I didn't want to go_____.

to that place

2. In the_____I will grow flowers.

the season after winter

3. The animals_____barking all night.

had been

4. The dog jumped_____of the window.

away from inside something

5. We_____get to school on time.

should; ought to

Check your answers with the key on page 70.

Home Again

PREPARATION

Key Words

basket	(bas´kit)	a woven box for carrying things *Put your flowers in this <u>basket</u>.*
don't	(dōnt)	do not *<u>Don't</u> hurry -- we will soon be there.*
no	(nō)	not so *<u>No</u>, Ann did not give me her money.*
ran	(ran)	went very fast on foot *Kim <u>ran</u> down the road.*
us	(us)	we; ourselves *He called <u>us</u> to come to supper.*

Home Again

Necessary Words

forget   (fər get´)   do not remember
        I sometimes <u>forget</u> to take my book.

held   (held)   kept a hold on; did not let go of
        She <u>held</u> the dog to keep it from running away.

rolls   (rōlz)   bread baked in little loaves
        We had <u>rolls</u> at supper last night.

sad   (sad)   unhappy
        She was <u>sad</u> that she lost her dog.

tired   (tīrd)   worn out
        Jenny was so <u>tired</u> she went to sleep.

Home Again

Heidi says good-by to Klara.

Preview: 1. Read the name of the story.
                2. Look at the picture.
                3. Read the sentence under the picture.
                4. Read the first three paragraphs of the story.
                5. Then answer the following question.
You learned from your preview that Heidi had a basket of rolls for
___a. Grandmother.
___b. Grandfather.
___c. Aunt Dete.
___d. Klara.

Turn to the Comprehension Check on page 46 for the right answer.

Now read the story.

Read to find out what Mr. Sesemann had put in the letter to Grandfather.

Home Again

The two girls were crying. Heidi was happy to be going home. But she was sad to say good-by to Klara.

She had a basket of rolls for Grandmother. She had a letter for Grandfather.

The girls said their last good-bys. "Don't forget us," Mr. Sesemann said.

Heidi held her basket all the way home.

She walked up the road. She came to Peter's house. She went in.

"I am back," she called. She was happy to see that Grandmother was not sick. "I have a basket of rolls for you."

Grandmother said, "Heidi! It is you! You are home! Sit here and talk to me."

"No, I don't have time now. I must go to Grandfather," Heidi said.

It was a long walk. Heidi was very tired when she got to Grandfather's house. Then she saw him and ran to him.

"Grandfather! Grandfather! I'm home. I missed you so much!"

He was so surprised, he could not say a word at first. Then he said, "Don't they want you? Have they sent you away?"

"No! They wanted me to stay. But I had to come home to you!" said Heidi.

He read the letter Heidi brought. Mr. Sesemann had sent money for Heidi.

At last Peter came, bringing the goats home. He saw Heidi and ran to the house.

"You are here!" cried Peter. "I am so happy you have come back to us!"

That night, Heidi did not walk in her sleep. She was back home, on the Alm. And she was happy.

Home Again

COMPREHENSION CHECK

Choose the best answer.

1. Klara was crying because
   _____a. she wanted to go to the Alm with Heidi.
   _____b. she wanted a basket of rolls too.
   _____c. Heidi would not be her friend anymore.
   _____d. she was going to miss Heidi.

2. When Heidi got to the Alm, where did she go first?
   _____a. To Grandfather's house.
   _____b. To Peter's house.
   _____c. To the top of the mountain to see the goats.
   _____d. To Aunt Dete's house.

3. Grandmother
   _____a. was afraid to let Heidi in.
   _____b. was very happy that Heidi was back.
   _____c. was very sad that Heidi was back.
   _____d. did not like the rolls Heidi had brought.

4. Grandfather's house
   _____a. was not close to Peter's house.
   _____b. was next door to Peter's house.
   _____c. was behind Peter's house.
   _____d. had been painted a new color.

5. When Heidi got to Grandfather's house
   _____a. she was hungry.
   _____b. she wanted a drink of water.
   _____c. she was dirty.
   _____d. she was tired.

6. Mr. Sesemann had sent Grandfather
   _____a. food for Heidi.
   _____b. clothes for Heidi.
   _____c. money for Heidi.
   _____d. books for Heidi to read.

7. Peter
   _____a. was angry at Heidi for leaving home.
   _____b. was angry that Heidi had so much money.
   _____c. was happy that Heidi had some money.
   _____d. was happy that Heidi had come home.

8. The first night back home, Heidi
   _____a. could not sleep.
   _____b. slept very well.
   _____c. cried for Klara.
   _____d. missed the kittens.

9. Another name for this story could be
   _____a. "Back On the Alm."
   _____b. "Rolls for Grandmother."
   _____c. "Heidi's Money."
   _____d. "Heidi Finds Peter."

10. This story is mainly about
    _____a. a young girl who was happy to be going home.
    _____b. a girl who was happy to leave her friend.
    _____c. a girl who had many friends.
    _____d. a girl who did not walk in her sleep.

Check your answers with the key on page 67.

This page may be reproduced for classroom use.

Home Again

VOCABULARY CHECK

basket	don't	no	ran	us

I. Sentences to Finish

Fill in the blank in each sentence with the correct key word from the box above.

1. I_____know how to tell time.

2. Jimmy_____fast to catch the ball.

3. My friend's mother will take_____to the circus.

4. We filled the_____with apples.

5. "_____, that is not what I told you."

II. Word Search

All the words from the box above are hidden in the puzzle below. They may be written from left to right, or up and down. As you find each word, put a circle around it. One word, that is not a key word, has been done for you.

```
B   A   S   N   E   D   D
A   X   F   D   U   O   O
S   R   U   O   V   N   O
B   A   S   K   E   T   U
T   N   G   W   F   S   P
```

Check your answers with the key on page 71.

This page may be reproduced for classroom use.

Helping Friends

PREPARATION

Key Words

box   (boks)   a holder to put things in
                         Give me that <u>box</u> of toys.

can't   (kant)   can not
                         We <u>can't</u> go to the park today.

each   (ēch)   every
                         <u>Each</u> day, they played ball.

tell   (tel)   talk about; make known to
                         Joan will <u>tell</u> Paul where we are.

too   (tü)   also
                         I am coming with you, <u>too</u>.

Helping Friends

Necessary Words

fields (fēldz) large, grassy places
The goats are in the <u>fields</u>.

gifts (giftz) presents
We are bringing birthday <u>gifts</u>.

month (munth) about 30 days
June went to the mountains for a <u>month</u>.

moved (müvd) went from one place to another
We <u>moved</u> to a new town last year.

together (tə geTH´ər) with another person or other people
Sue and Ted ate supper <u>together</u>.

Helping Friends

Dr. Classen brings gifts to Heidi.

Preview: 1. Read the name of the story.
2. Look at the picture.
3. Read the sentence under the picture.
4. Read the first four paragraphs of the story.
5. Then answer the following question.

You learned from your preview that Klara wanted to

___a. go to the doctor.
___b. see Peter and the goats.
___c. see Grandmother.
___d. go see Heidi.

Turn to the Comprehension Check on page 52 for the right answer.

Now read the story.

Read to find out how Heidi helped Peter to read.

Helping Friends

Klara wanted to go see Heidi on the Alm.

"She can't go," said Dr. Classen. "I know how much she wants to. But she is a sick little girl. Tell her that she may go in the spring."

"You must go in her place, old friend," said Mr. Sesemann. You are tired. It will be good for you. You can take a box of gifts to Heidi. You can tell us all about the Alm, too."

Heidi was surprised when Dr. Classen came. "But where are Klara and Grandmamma?" she asked.

"Klara is coming in the spring," said Dr. Classen. "I have a box of things she sent to you."

The next day, Dr. Classen and Heidi went to Peter's house. Klara had sent gifts for Grandmother, too. Together, they went up the Alm to look for Peter and the goats.

Dr. Classen had never seen such a beautiful place. He and Heidi walked in the green fields. They looked at the mountains. He was tired and sad when he came. But now, he was much better.

Dr. Classen stayed for one month. Each day, he went for a walk on the Alm. He talked to Grandfather about it.

Winter was coming. Dr. Classen went home. But Heidi knew he would come back one day.

Then one day, Grandfather and Heidi left the mountains. They moved to town at the bottom of the Alm. There was a school in town. And Grandfather wanted Heidi to go there.

Peter came to see Heidi after school. Peter was not doing well. He could not read.

"You must learn," said Heidi.

"Can't," said Peter.

"Klara sent me a book," Heidi said. "We will use it to help you learn."

Each day, they worked. Peter worked very hard. Soon he could read as well as the other children at school.

Helping Friends

COMPREHENSION CHECK

Choose the best answer.

Preview Answer:

d. go see Heidi.

1. Klara wanted to go to the Alm because
   _____a. she wanted to see the goats.
   _____b. she missed her friend.
   _____c. she wanted to bring rolls to Peter's grandmother.
   _____d. she had gifts for Heidi.

2. Dr. Classen said that Klara could go to the Alm
   _____a. when she could walk.
   _____b. when she stopped crying.
   _____c. when she finished her lessons.
   _____d. in the spring.

3. Mr. Sesemann
   _____a. sent Dr. Classen to the Alm.
   _____b. sent Grandmamma to the Alm .
   _____c. sent Miss Rottenmeier to the Alm.
   _____d. sent the kittens to the Alm.

4. Klara had sent gifts with Dr. Classen for
   _____a. Heidi.
   _____b. Grandmother.
   _____c. Heidi and Grandmother.
   _____d. Peter.

5. Dr. Classen thought the Alm was
   _____a. a cold place.
   _____b. a beautiful place.
   _____c. a dark place.
   _____d. a great place for goats.

6. Dr. Classen stayed on the Alm for
   _____a. one week.
   _____b. one month.
   _____c. one year.
   _____d. three days.

7. Grandfather and Heidi moved from the Alm so that
   _____a. Heidi could be near the stores.
   _____b. Heidi could see Aunt Dete.
   _____c. Heidi could have more friends.
   _____d. Heidi could go to school.

8. Heidi helped Peter
   _____a. learn how to read.
   _____b. learn how to dress.
   _____c. learn how to talk.
   _____d. make new friends.

9. Another name for this story could be
   _____a. "Gifts for Heidi."
   _____b. "Leaving the Alm."
   _____c. "Heidi Helps Peter Learn."
   _____d. "A Pretty Place in the Mountains."

10. This story is mainly about
    _____a. how Heidi helps her friend Peter.
    _____b. Dr. Classen's trip to the Alm.
    _____c. why Klara sent gifts to the Alm.
    _____d. why Heidi moved to town.

Check your answers with the key on page 67.

This page may be reproduced for classroom use.

Helping Friends

VOCABULARY CHECK

box	can't	each	tell	too

I. Sentences to Finish

Fill in the blank in each sentence with the correct key word from the box above.

1. "Mother, please_____me a story."

2. Alice gave_____of us a cookie.

3. I opened the_____to see what was inside.

4. If you_____come over now, please come later.

5. Maria has a new dress. Her sister Lizzy has one_____.

II. Crossword Puzzle

Use the words from the box above to fill in the puzzle. Use the meanings to help you choose the right answer.

ACROSS
2. every
4. also

DOWN
1. talk about; make known to
3. can not
5. a holder to put things in

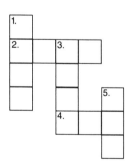

Check your answers with the key on page 71.

This page may be reproduced for classroom use.

On the Alm

PREPARATION

Key Words

color   (kul´ər)   a tint such as yellow, red, or green
The <u>color</u> of May's dress is red.

from   (from)   Take the ball <u>from</u> him. He came <u>from</u> Mars.
Bring something <u>from</u> home.

if   (if)   in the event that
I will play ball with you <u>if</u> I have time.

lunch   (lunch)   the noon meal
They will eat <u>lunch</u> in the car.

yellow   (yel´ō)   the color of the sun
Our school bus is <u>yellow</u>.

On the Alm

Necessary Words

excited	(ek sīt´id)	turned on; filled with joy
		They were <u>excited</u> about going on the boat.
eyes	(īz)	parts of the body you see with
		Peggy has blue <u>eyes</u>.
forgot	(fər got´)	did not remember
		I <u>forgot</u> my lunch money.
hugged	(hugd)	held on to tightly
		Joy <u>hugged</u> her mother.
later	(lāt´ər)	a little after that time
		We said we would see them <u>later</u>.

On the Alm

Heidi learns that Klara and Grandmamma are coming to the Alm!

Preview: 1. Read the name of the story.
                2. Look at the picture.
                3. Read the sentence under the picture.
                4. Read the first three paragraphs of the story.
                5. Then answer the following question.
You learned from your preview that Heidi got a letter from
___a. Grandmother.
___b. Klara.
___c. Mr. Sesemann.
___d. Miss Rottenmeier.

Turn to the Comprehension Check on page 58 for the right answer.

Now read the story.

Read to find out how long Klara will stay with Heidi.

On the Alm

Spring had come. Winter was gone from the mountains. Heidi and Grandfather moved again. They went back to their house on the Alm.

One day, Peter brought a letter. It was a letter from Klara. He put it in the bag with his lunch. He forgot to give it to Heidi. Later, he found it. He gave it to her.

Heidi read the letter. It said that Klara and Grandmamma were coming.

Peter and his grandmother did not like this. What if Heidi went back to the city with them?

Then, one morning, Heidi saw people coming up the Alm. It was them! Some men carried Klara in a chair. Grandmamma was riding a horse.

Heidi and Grandfather met them.

Klara was excited and happy. "Oh, Heidi! It is just as you said! The Alm is so beautiful. There are flowers of every color. Beautiful colors!--- Blue and red and yellow!"

"Grandfather calls the yellow ones 'sun's eyes'," Heidi said.

They had lunch at Grandfather's house. Klara ate and ate. "This is so good," she said. "At home, I never wanted to eat."

Later, Grandfather talked to Grandmamma. "Let Klara stay here. Just for a time," he said. "We will look after her. If you will let her stay, it may do her good."

"I think so too," said Grandmamma.

The girls were excited. How long could Klara stay?

"A month," said Grandmamma. "In a month, we will know. Let us see if staying on the Alm helps Klara."

The girls hugged. They would have a month together, on the Alm!

On the Alm

COMPREHENSION CHECK

Choose the best answer.

Preview Answer:
b. Klara.

1. When spring came, Heidi and Grandfather
   ____a. went to see Klara.
   ____b. moved back to the Alm.
   ____c. went to see Grandmamma.
   ____d. started a garden.

2. One day Peter brought Heidi
   ____a. a goat of her own.
   ____b. a new dress.
   ____c. a gift for her birthday.
   ____d. a letter from Klara.

3. The letter said that
   ____a. Klara could not come to the Alm.
   ____b. Klara wanted Heidi to come see her.
   ____c. Klara and Grandmamma were coming.
   ____d. Klara and Dr. Classen were coming.

4. Peter and his grandmother were afraid that Klara and Grandmamma
   ____a. would not like the Alm.
   ____b. would take Heidi back to the city.
   ____c. would not like Peter.
   ____d. would be afraid of the goats.

5. Peter and his grandmother
   ____a. did not like Klara.
   ____b. did not like Grandmamma.
   ____c. did not like Miss Rottenmeier.
   ____d. loved Heidi.

6. Klara thought the Alm
   ____a. was not a pretty place.
   ____b. was very beautiful.
   ____c. was not a friendly place.
   ____d. was the last place anyone would want to live.

7. On the Alm, Klara
   ____a. started to eat better.
   ____b. cried every night.
   ____c. got very sick.
   ____d. began to miss *her* home.

8. Grandmamma said that Klara could stay on the Alm for
   ____a. ten days.
   ____b. ten years.
   ____c. one month.
   ____d. one week.

9. Another name for this story could be
   ____a. "Klara Comes to the Alm."
   ____b. "Leaving Town."
   ____c. "The Sun's Eyes."
   ____d. "Grandmamma Rides a Horse."

10. This story is mainly about
   ____a. a sick young girl who gets better on the Alm.
   ____b. why Peter and his grandmother did not like Klara.
   ____c. two friends who are happy to be together again.
   ____d. winter on the mountains.

Check your answers with the key on page 67.

On the Alm

VOCABULARY CHECK

color	from	if	lunch	yellow

I. Sentences to Finish
Fill in the blank in each sentence with the correct key word from the box above.

1. Tammy will_____the picture green.

2. After_____, we can go out to play.

3. Please let me know _____you can come to my party.

4. When bananas are ready to pick, they are_____.

5. I heard_____ grandma yesterday.

II. Using the Words
On the lines below, write five of your own sentences using the key words from the box above. Use each word once, drawing a line under the key word.

1. _____

2. _____

3. _____

4. _____

5. _____

Check your answers with the key on page 71

This page may be reproduced for classroom use.

The Lost Wheel Chair

PREPARATION

Key Words

by   (bī)   next to; beside
> *They saw a cow <u>by</u> the road.*

lost   (lôst)   gone for good; not able to be found
> *I <u>lost</u> my best hat.*

or   (ôr)   a word that marks a choice
> *You may have cake <u>or</u> cookies.*

sat   (sat)   rested on the bottom
> *Seth <u>sat</u> on the grass.*

three   (thrē)   the number 3; one more after two
> *They saw <u>three</u> fish in the water.*

The Lost Wheel Chair

Necessary Words

himself   (him self´)   he
Tom did the work <u>himself</u>.

hurt   (hėrt)   cause pain
You may <u>hurt</u> your hand on that saw.

left   (left)   went away from
We <u>left</u> the house around noon.

push   (pu̇sh)   cause to move
We will <u>push</u> his car to make it go.

wonderful   (wun´dər fəl)   great
This is a <u>wonderful</u> place for a party.

The Lost Wheel Chair

Peter waited until no one was looking. Then he pushed Klara's wheel chair off the mountain.

Preview: 1. Read the name of the story.
                   2. Look at the picture.
                   3. Read the sentences under the picture.
                   4. Read the first two paragraphs of the story.
                   5. Then answer the following question.

You learned from your preview that Peter

___a. pushed Klara's wheel chair up the mountain.

___b. pushed Klara's wheel chair off the mountain.

___c. fell down the mountain.

___d. rattled the mountain.

Turn to the Comprehension Check on page 64 for the right answer.

Now read the story.

Read to find out what happened to Klara one day on the mountain.

The Lost Wheel Chair

Peter was angry. Heidi was always with Klara. He wanted to have her all to himself.

One day, he saw that Klara's wheel chair was left by the door. He looked around. No one was near to see him. He gave the wheel chair a push. One, two, three! It rattled down the mountain!

Klara's chair was lost. Heidi guessed that the wind had pushed it down the mountain.

"I must have my chair. Or I will have to go home," Klara said.

"No," said Grandfather. "I can carry you." And that is what he did. When Peter would come for the goats, Grandfather would carry Klara up the mountain to be with Heidi and Peter. Later, he would come back to carry Klara down.

One day, as Klara sat in the grass, she cried. Now that her chair was lost, she sat in one place. She could not move around.

"There are such beautiful flowers here by me," Heidi said. "Peter and I will carry you over."

Peter and Heidi did their best to carry Klara. But the three children had a hard time.

"Put your feet down on the ground, Klara," said Heidi. "Try to stand."

Klara tried. "I can do it! I can stand! It does not hurt!" She took a step alone. With each step, she did a little better.

"Look! I can walk! I can walk!" Klara cried.

"Now you don't need a chair *or* Grandfather to carry you," said Heidi.

Days had passed. Grandmamma came back. She was happy to see Klara walking. Then Mr. Sesemann came. He could not believe his eyes when he saw Klara.

"This is wonderful! How can I thank you?" he said to Grandfather. "My Klara is walking!"

Soon, it was time for Klara to go home. The girls were sad. But they knew that Klara would be coming again next year, to Heidi's home on the beautiful Alm.

The Lost Wheel Chair

COMPREHENSION CHECK

Choose the best answer.

(1.) Peter pushed Klara's wheel chair off the mountain thinking that
_____a. Klara would have to learn how to walk.
_____b. Klara would not want to stay anymore.
_____c. without her wheel chair, she would have
_____ to go home.
_____d. she would buy a better one.

2. Heidi thought
_____a. that someone had taken Klara's wheel chair.
_____b. the wind had pushed the wheel chair down the mountain.
_____c. that Klara forgot where she left her chair.
_____d. that Grandfather sold the chair.

3. Grandfather did not want Klara to go home, so he
_____a. carried her where she needed to go.
_____b. bought her a new wheel chair.
_____c. found and fixed her broken wheel chair.
_____d. asked Mr. Sesemann to send Klara a new chair.

4. One day Klara sat in the grass, crying. Why?
_____a. She missed her wheel chair.
_____b. She missed her home in the city.
_____c. She missed her Grandmamma.
_____d. She could not move around without her chair.

5. Peter and Heidi tried their best to
_____a. find Klara's wheel chair.
_____b. fix Klara's wheel chair.
_____c. make Klara laugh.
_____d. carry Klara over to where they were sitting.

6. One day when Klara put her feet down,
_____a. it did not hurt for her to stand.
_____b. it hurt so much that she cried.
_____c. she fell to the ground.
_____d. she stepped on Peter's foot.

7. With each step Klara took,
_____a. she cried a little more.
_____b. she did a little better.
_____c. she became more afraid.
_____d. she became more tired.

8. Mr. Sesemann could not believe his eyes when he saw
_____a. Klara's broken wheel chair.
_____b. all the goats.
_____c. Klara smiling.
_____d. Klara walking.

9. Another name for this story could be
_____a. "On Her Feet Again."
_____b. "Peter's Dirty Trick."
_____c. "Klara Leaves the Alm."
_____d. "Heidi Loses a Friend."

10. This story is mainly about
_____a. how the Alm and Heidi helped a little girl to walk again.
_____b. why Peter pushed Klara's wheel chair off the mountain.
_____c. the beautiful flowers on the Alm.
_____d. why Mr. Sesemann thanked Grandfather.

Check your answers with the key on page 67.

This page may be reproduced for classroom use.

The Lost Wheel Chair

VOCABULARY CHECK

by	lost	or	sat	three

I. Sentences to Finish

Fill in the blank in each sentence with the correct key word from the box above.

1. I_____next to Kim on the bus today.

2. I left my book on the grass_____the swing.

3. Mother gave me_____cookies.

4. My brother_____his ring this morning.

5. Should I try this one_____the other one?

II. Matching

Write the letter of the correct meaning from Column B next to the key word in Column A.

Column A	Column B
_____1. by	a. a word that marks a choice
_____2. lost	b. the number 3; one more after two
_____3. or	c. next to; beside
_____4. sat	d. gone for good; not able to be found
_____5. three	e. rested on the bottom

Check your answers with the key on page 72.

This page may be reproduced for classroom use.

NOTES

COMPREHENSION CHECK PROGRESS CHART
Lessons CTR A-61 to CTR A-70

LESSON NUMBER	QUESTION NUMBER										PAGE NUMBER
	1	2	3	4	5	6	7	8	9	10	
CTR A-61	d	b	(b)	c	a	a	d	b	△b	□a	10
CTR A-62	d	a	a	a	b	b	d	(b)	△a	□c	16
CTR A-63	c	c	(a)	d	b	b	a	d	△b	□a	22
CTR A-64	(d)	c	d	a	b	b	a	d	△a	□c	28
CTR A-65	(c)	c	b	d	c	a	d	b	△a	□a	34
CTR A-66	d	d	(c)	(a)	b	b	c	d	△c	□d	40
CTR A-67	(d)	b	(b)	(a)	d	c	d	(b)	△a	□a	46
CTR A-68	(b)	d	a	c	b	b	d	a	△c	□a	52
CTR A-69	b	d	c	b	(d)	b	a	c	△a	□c	58
CTR A-70	(c)	b	a	d	d	a	b	d	△a	□a	64

◯ = Inference (not said straight out, but you know from what is said)

△ = Another name for the story

□ = Main idea of the story

NOTES

VOCABULARY CHECK ANSWER KEY
Lessons CTR A-61 to CTR A-70

61   GRANDFATHER'S HOUSE   **11**

I. 1. happy   *II.* 1. NO
     2. new   2. YES
     3. your   3. YES
     4. looked   4. NO
     5. was   5. YES

62   PETER   **17**

I. 1. her
     2. eat
     3. are
     4. sit
     5. goat

63   HEIDI MEETS KLARA   **23**

I. 1. living   *II.* 1. c
     2. be   2. d
     3. read   3. b
     4. ask   4. a
     5. call   5. e

VOCABULARY CHECK ANSWER KEY
Lessons CTR A-61 to CTR A-70

64   **KITTENS FOR KLARA**   29

I. 1. after
    2. bring
    3. pocket
    4. kitten
    5. could

II. 1. c
     2. e
     3. d
     4. a
     5. b

65   **HEIDI'S BOOK**   35

I. 1. pleasure
    2. picture
    3. of
    4. am
    5. has

II.

```
A  C  D  P  L  E  A  S  E
M  P  L  I  Q  R  F  C  O
H  B  O  C  H  I  N  E  F
A  H  G  T  A  X  M  A  A
T  A  H  U  S  V  O  L  R
U  E  L  R  N  G  Z  Q  T
S  T  T  E  X  P  P  O  B
```

66   **THE OPEN DOOR**   41

I. 1. there
    2. were
    3. must
    4. spring
    5. out

II. 1. there
     2. spring
     3. were
     4. out
     5. must

VOCABULARY CHECK ANSWER KEY
Lessons CTR A-61 to CTR A-70

LESSON NUMBER

PAGE NUMBER

67   **HOME AGAIN**   **47**

I. 1. don't
      2. ran
      3. us
      4. basket
      5. No

II.

68   **HELPING FRIENDS**   **53**

I. 1. tell
      2. each
      3. box
      4. can't
      5. too

II.

```
¹T
²E  A  ³C  H
L      A
L      N      ⁵B
       ⁴T  O  O
              X
```

69   **ON THE ALM**   **59**

I. 1. color
      2. lunch
      3. if
      4. yellow
      5. from

VOCABULARY CHECK ANSWER KEY
Lessons CTR A-61 to CTR A-70

I.   1. sat   *II.*   1. c
     2. by   2. d
     3. three   3. a
     4. lost   4. e
     5. or   5. b